THE UGLY DUCKLING

Illustrated by Amelia Rosato

Retold by Rita Storey

PUFFIN BOOKS

A long time ago in a field by a river sat a duck, patiently waiting for her eggs to hatch.

At last, one by one, the eggs cracked and out popped five, pretty, little duckling heads . . .

followed by five, pretty, little duckling bodies.

But the biggest egg of them all had not cracked . . .

so rather impatiently the duck settled herself down again with a sigh, to keep it warm.

She waited . . .

and waited . . .

and waited . . .

until at last the big egg cracked . . .

and out came a very large and very ugly duckling head, followed by a big and even uglier duckling body . . .

and even larger and very ugly duckling feet. The mother duck was horrified!

The next day the mother duck took her children for a swim. With a quack she jumped in . . .

and one . . .   by one . . .   the ducklings followed . . .

even the ugly duckling who . . .

with his large feet, was a better swimmer than his brothers and sisters.

The mother duck took them to meet the
rest of the animals in the farmyard.

The Spanish chicken, who was very important,
clucked approvingly . . .

until she saw the ugly duckling.

Oh dear me!

The turkey, who was emperor of the farmyard, gobbled with pleasure . . .

until he saw the ugly duckling.

The ugly duckling was very sad.

Everyone laughed at him.

No one would talk to him.

He desperately wanted to be handsome.
He hated his feet, they were too big.

He hated his feathers,
they were so shabby.

He hated his wings,
they were too small.

So one day he ran away.

He ran out of the farmyard . . .

and over the moors where the wild ducks lived.

Through the deep, dark forest . . .

he walked . . . and walked . . . and walked.

Sometimes other animals attacked him.

Sometimes they laughed at him. He was very lonely and frightened.

Tired of travelling, the ugly duckling made his home by a lake but when winter came it began to freeze up. The hole in which the duckling was swimming got smaller . . .

and smaller . . .

and smaller . . .

until the duckling could no longer swim . . .

and froze fast in the ice.

A farm worker walking past saw him.

He broke the ice and carried him home to his family.

Everyone was very kind but the duckling
was frightened.

He fluttered his wings to try and fly away and knocked over a bowl of milk . . .

the milk went everywhere.

The little boy tried to catch him but he flew away and fell into a butter churn . . .

he clambered out . . .

only to fall straight into a barrel of oats. The kitchen was in chaos, the children were laughing, the mother screamed and there were milk and oats all over the place.

The terrified duckling saw
an open door and ran out.

He ran until he could go no further and then hid among the reeds. There he stayed for the rest of the winter.

The winter turned to spring and the duckling looked out of his hiding place to see three swans swimming on the lake.

The swans saw him and swam over to him. He hung his head in shame. Why should such lovely birds be friends with him? As he did so he saw their reflections in the water . . .

but to his amazement instead of three beautiful swans looking back at him there were four.

The little, bedraggled, ugly duckling who nobody loved had turned into the most handsome swan of them all!
He was no longer the ugly duckling. And he was amongst friends at last!

The end